Lisa Olmos

202
363-4702

Dec 1982

I AM FOUR

I AM FOUR

LOUISE FITZHUGH

with pictures by
Susan Bonners

DELACORTE PRESS / NEW YORK

Published by
Delacorte Press
1 Dag Hammarskjold Plaza
New York, N.Y. 10017

Manufactured in the United States of America

First Printing

Library of Congress Cataloging in Publication Data

Fitzhugh, Louise.
I am four.

Summary: Describes the activities and
accomplishments of a typical four-year-old.
I. Bonners, Susan, ill. II. Title.
PZ7.F5768Ian 1982   [E]   82-70309
ISBN 0-440-03972-X   AACR2
ISBN 0-440-03973-8 (lib. bdg.)

Other books by Louise Fitzhugh

Harriet the Spy
The Long Secret
Sport
Nobody's Family Is Going to Change
I Am Five
I Am Three

I am four.

I run away with myself.

I like to discuss.
I would now like to
discuss farms.

I eike to discuss "fish".

Lisa could draw forever.
Rainbows, dark rooms with balls +
stripes

I could draw on

+ beautiful things in it

I like to draw + I like to a

Lisa loves to make

Valentines Cards

I like to paint

and on

and on

and on.

Can I
set the table?

Yes

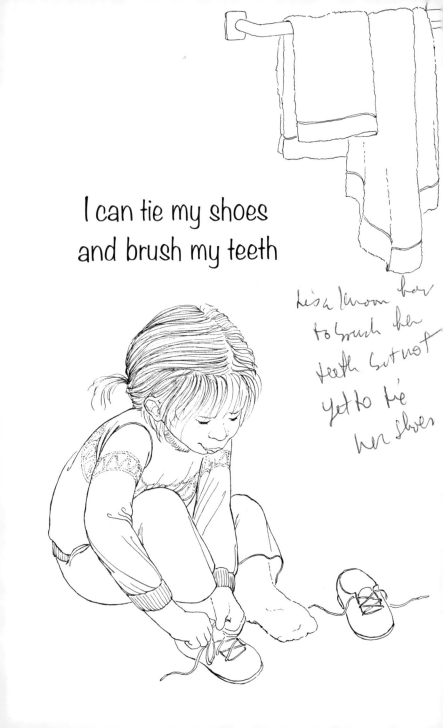

I can tie my shoes
and brush my teeth

Lisa known how
to brush her
teeth but not
yet to tie
her shoes

and hop.

I'm a very good
 hopper.

Lisa is a vy good hoppe
 + dancer.
 She goes to ballet lessons

Tomorrow a big monster dragged me by my legs and I struggled to let go. It was really my father!

Yesterday a lion
almost ate me up
as I came into
the living room!

Sometimes I look at somebody else & I see that I'm bigger.

I'm bigger than
you are. I'm so much
bigger, it's not funny.
I can throw you out of
the house I'm so much
bigger!

SANTA CLAUS!

Now I can finish things!

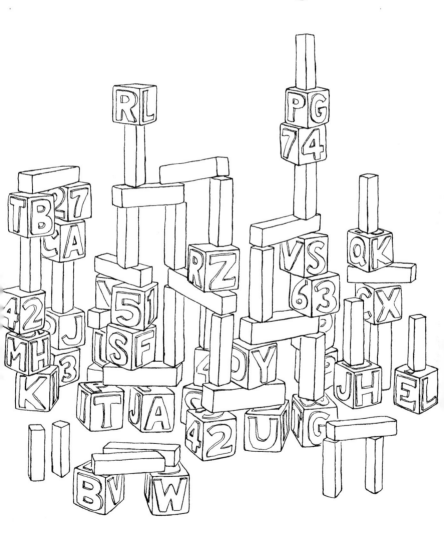

I just don't
like to HEAR
fire engines.

Lisa doesn't like
my seeing noises either.

What does
my back look like?

Lisa loves to play dress ups

Sometimes

I just fling myself about
for the fun of it.

Is that real?

Lisa likes unicorns.
Kerry Kash saw a real unicorn.
But I haven't.
I saw a camel that is
real.

To be four years old:
I get sad a very long time when my parents
are mad at me.
They don't like the   things I have done
they think I've ruined   their life.
Every day I can   read a book
and I love ready   books.
I have togs   and I know
how to weave   and it's
fun to weave.
I like Going to school   and hay
snacks when I'm hungry.

That's all about me.

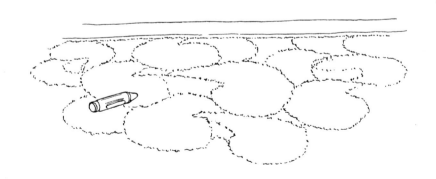

ABOUT THE AUTHOR

LOUISE FITZHUGH's delightful series about growing up includes *I Am Three, I Am Four,* and *I Am Five.* Born in Memphis, Tennessee, in 1928, the author was a multitalented person. She studied painting at the Art Students League in New York City and in Bologna, Italy, and was widely recognized as an artist. Her best-known novels, *Harriet the Spy* and *The Long Secret,* have become international best sellers. She wrote *I Am Four* before her death in 1974.

ABOUT THE ARTIST

SUSAN BONNERS was born in Chicago and was graduated from Fordham University. She has illustrated many books for children, among them *Panda* and *A Penguin Year,* both chosen as Notable Books by the American Library Association. *A Penguin Year* was a winner of the American Book Award in 1982. Ms. Bonners lives in Brooklyn, New York.

ABOUT THE BOOK

The illustrations for *I Am Four* were prepared in ink, and the cover was done in watercolor. It was printed by The Maple-Vail Book Manufacturing Group and bound by A. Horowitz & Sons, Bookbinders.